This Book Belongs to

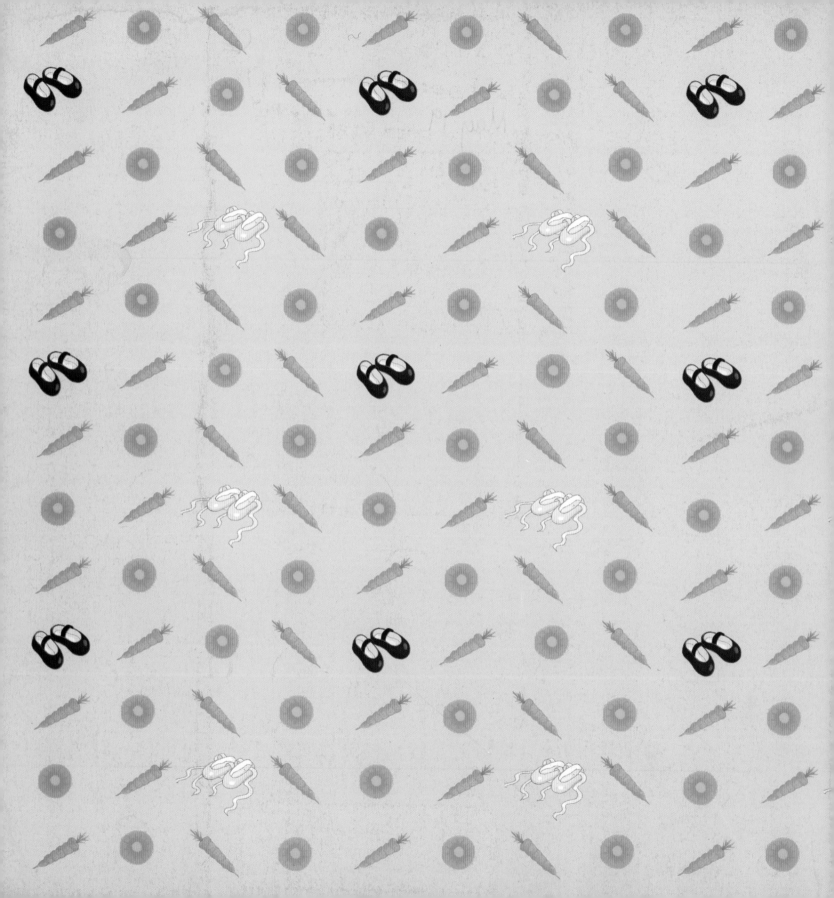

Text and illustrations copyright © Judy Brown 2019

First published in Great Britain and in the USA in 2019 by
Otter-Barry Books, Little Orchard, Burley Gate, Herefordshire, HR1 3QS
www.otterbarrybooks.com

ISBN 978-1-910959-33-6

Illustrated with mixed media

Set in Trebuchet

Printed in China

9 8 7 6 5 4 3 2 1

Bruno and Bella

THE DANCE CLASS

Judy Brown

Otter-Barry BOOKS

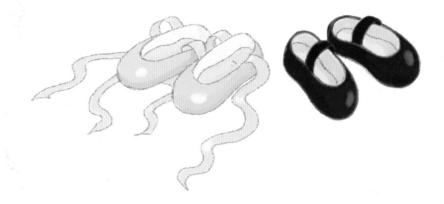

Bella wanted to learn to dance.

"Let's join the class!" she said.

Bruno wasn't sure
if he wanted to go.

They both went along.
The first week they did ballet.

Bella wasn't very
good at ballet.

The second week they did ballroom dancing.

Bella had a bit of trouble with ballroom dancing.

The third week
was tap dancing.

Tap dancing was a disaster.

Things didn't get any better
after that.

Bella told the teacher she wasn't going to come to Dance Class any more.

Bella was upset.

"I wish I was better at dancing," she said.
"I wanted to be in the show."

"Maybe you could join a different class," said Bruno.

Bella waited outside
and watched the others dance.

Bella was bored.

But then she spotted something interesting.

She went to see what was going on.

It was an Art Class and it looked like they were having fun.

"Come and join us!"
said the teacher.

So Bella did. She loved it!

A few weeks later, Bella's paintings were
on display for everyone to see.

Bella didn't mind that she wasn't in the show — she **loved** watching it.

And Bruno…

...Bruno danced a solo!

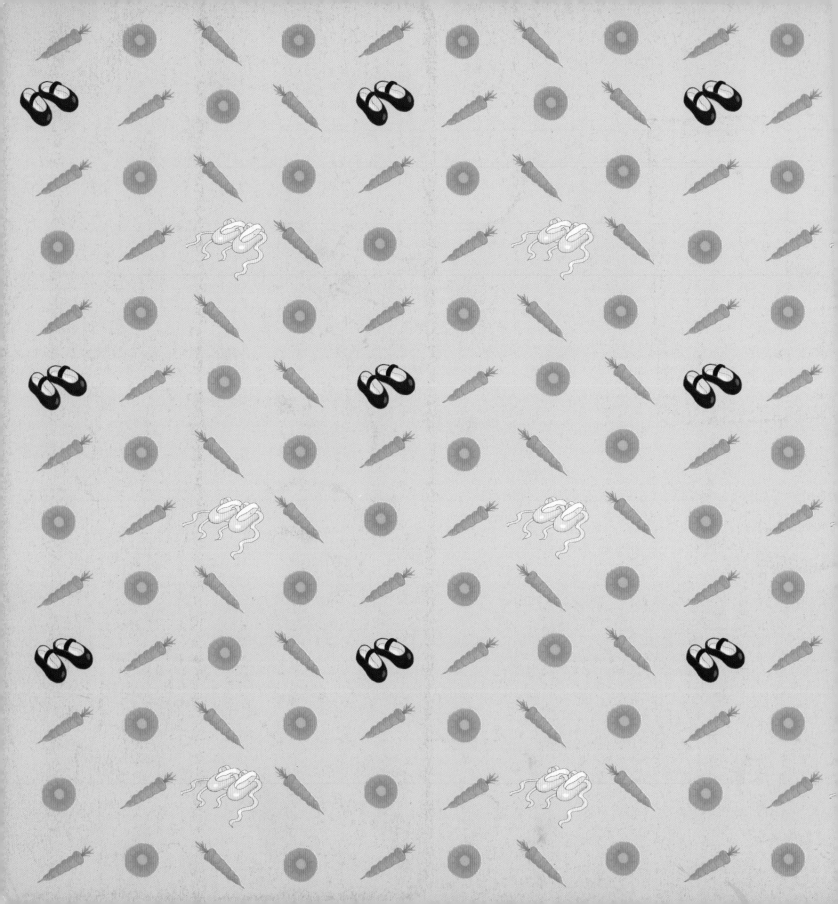

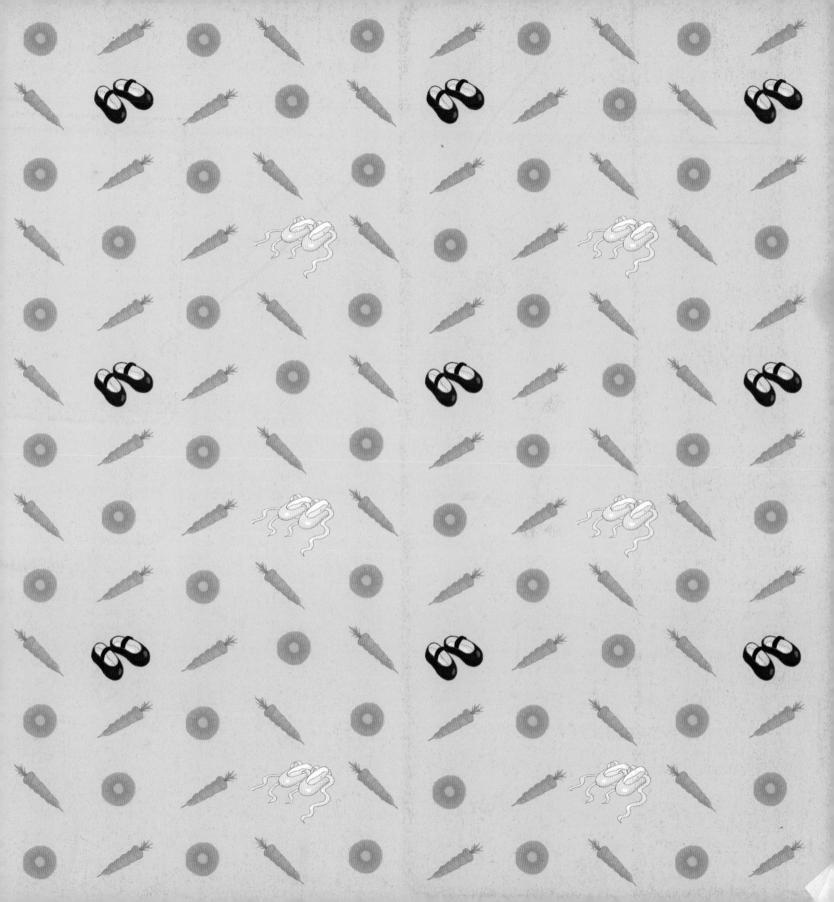

ABOUT THE AUTHOR

Judy Brown has written and illustrated three popular series of children's story books: *Pirate Princess*, *Super Soccer Boy* and *Petbots*. *Bruno and Bella* is her first preschool picture book series, and was inspired by being a mum to her own very different twin girl and boy. The books were created using both traditional and digital media. Judy Brown lives in Surrey with her husband, children and two skinny cats, and when she's not writing or illustrating, she's playing violin, making jewellery or pottering around in her garden workshop.